The Trout Fishing Song

Written by Jeanne Willis

Illustrated by Clare Elsom

"Cast out," said Scout. "Cast out now for a trout."

"The line's out," said Cowboy. "Shout out for that trout."

Cowboys shout loudly but scouts can shout louder.

"Look out!" shouted Scout. "There's a trout! There's a trout!"

"That trout," shouted Scout, "is around and about. Around and about with a hook in its mouth!"

"We should cook up that trout," said
Cowboy to Scout. "We should hook it and
cook it and fry it in oil."

Said Scout, "We must hook it and cook it in foil."

"Fry me in oil? It is too hot!" spouted Trout.
"Cook me in foil? I will not stand the heat!"

"Try something different. Try oysters I beg you. Oysters are many times sweeter to eat."

Alas for our boys, Trout spat the hook out.
Alas for our boys, Trout went on his way.

Were our boys annoyed? No, they both enjoyed oysters.
So sweet and so different they ate them all day!